Green Shamrocks

To Dianne Gibb, who comes from the land of shamrocks.
~E. B.

To Maude, Anne, and Lou. Three lovely, funny, bouncy little bunnies.
With love, Jojo

Text copyright © 2011 by Eve Bunting.
Illustrations copyright © 2011 by Joëlle Dreidemy.

All rights reserved. Published by Scholastic Inc.
SCHOLASTIC, CARTWHEEL BOOKS, and associated logos are trademarks and/or registered trademarks of Scholastic Inc.

Library of Congress Cataloging-in-Publication Data is available.

ISBN 978-0-545-27443-2

10 9 8 7 6 5 4 3 2 1   11 12 13 14 15

Printed in the U.S.A.   08
First printing, January 2011

Green Shamrocks

Eve Bunting

Joëlle Dreidemy

Cartwheel
·B·O·O·K·S· ®

Scholastic Inc.

New York   Toronto   London   Auckland
Sydney   Mexico City   New Delhi   Hong Kong

Rabbit marked the last day of February on his calendar. Tomorrow would be March. Soon it would be

St. Patrick's Day!

Rabbit had a packet of shamrock seeds.
"I will grow my own shamrocks for the
special day," he said.
"I can wear them to the St. Patrick's Day parade.
But what can I grow them in?"

Rabbit went looking.

He found a yellow pot under a tree.
"This will be **perfect**," he said.
He rolled the pot all the way home.

He filled it with earth

and sowed his shamrock seeds.

He clapped his paws and smiled. "They will be ready in good time for St. Patrick's Day," he said.

Each day he watered his shamrocks.

He moved the pot to make sure they got sun and shade.

And the little seedlings grew **stronger**.

Soon the green leaves spread across the yellow pot.
The shamrocks were ready!

Rabbit clapped his paws and smiled.
"Tomorrow is St. Patrick's Day. I will make
a shamrock chain. It will be perfect."

He went to bed and dreamed of the parade.

But when he got up in the morning, his yellow pot of green shamrocks was gone.

"Oh, no!" he moaned.

"Did **YOU** take my yellow pot of green shamrocks?" he asked Squirrel.

"No," Squirrel said. "Try Woodchuck. I saw him come out of his burrow this morning."

"Woodchuck, did **YOU** take my yellow pot of green shamrocks? I need them for the parade."

"No," Woodchuck said. "Try Goat. Goat eats everything. He probably ate your yellow pot of green shamrocks."

"Oh, no!" Rabbit closed his eyes. "Oh, no!" He ran fast to Goat's house.

"Goat? Did **YOU** take my yellow pot of green shamrocks?"
"**No**," Goat said.

"I have a yellow pot of green shamrocks. But they are mine. A big wind came last night. The wind gave them to me. He blew them in my open door."

Rabbit peeked in Goat's open door.
There was a yellow pot of green shamrocks on Goat's table. And a plate and a fork and a knife.

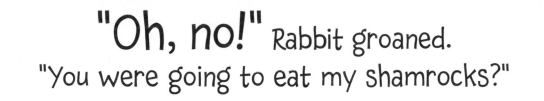

"Oh, no!" Rabbit groaned.
"You were going to eat my shamrocks?"

"Indeed, no," Goat said. "I do not like green salad for breakfast. I am having this nice tin can and this chewy rubber ball. Would you care to join me?"

"Thanks," Rabbit said. "But all I want are my green shamrocks. They are mine. I grew them all spring."

"But how can I give away a gift? I know! I will give you the shamrocks. All I want is the yellow pot."

Goat pulled the green shamrocks from the yellow pot and handed them to Rabbit.

"Oh, **thank you**," Rabbit said.

"I plan to wear the shamrocks to the parade."

"And I plan to wear the yellow pot," Goat said.

"Really?" Rabbit clapped his paws.
"We can go together."

Rabbit sat at Goat's table and made his shamrock chain.

He hung it around his neck.

Goat perched the yellow pot
on his head.

They linked arms and set off.

The parade was just starting.

There were **bands** and **marchers** and **balloons**.

There was a rabbit wearing a green shamrock chain and a goat wearing a yellow pot on his head.

"Happy St. Patrick's Day!" they called out
to everyone they met.

"Happy St. Patrick's Day to you!"

3/23/16 Book is stained on top
outer corner from front to back.
WGRL-HQSC